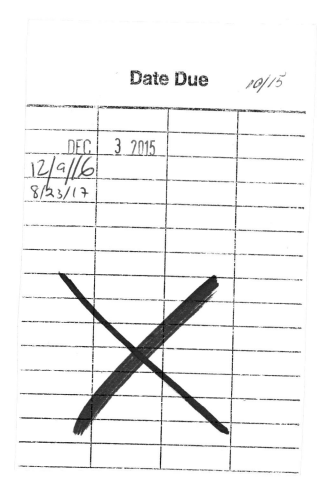

Date Due 10/15

DEC 3 2015
12/9/16
8/23/17

For my wonderful son-in-law, Art,
and my precious, playful grandson,
Peter McKinney Min ~ M. M.

For Tom the Mule, Ian the Dog, and Simon B Snake—
a real bunch of animals! ~ S. J.

tiger tales
5 River Road, Suite 128, Wilton, CT 06897
Published in the United States 2015
Originally published in Great Britain 2015
by Little Tiger Press
Text copyright © 2015 Marni McGee
Illustrations copyright © 2015 Sean Julian
ISBN-13: 978-1-58925-189-2
ISBN-10: 1-58925-189-X
Printed in China
LTP/1400/1142/0315

For more insight and activities,
visit us at www.tigertalesbooks.com

Bear Can't Sleep!

by Marni McGee

Illustrated by Sean Julian

tiger tales

It was winter, and all the animals were busy. Soon the forest would be covered in snow.

Fox gathered wood for winter fires, while Owl and Squirrel made pickles and jam.

Patch the Hare tried to help, but he got in everyone's way—as usual.

Whoops!

"Oh, get your feet
out of my berries!"
cried Squirrel.

"Listen," hooted Owl.
"What's that strange sound?"

Peeking around the trees, the animals saw a huge, grumbly bear dragging branches behind him.

Everyone froze, except Patch.

"Hey, Mr. Bear!" he shouted.
"Need some help?"

He's as big as a mountain.

He's heading for the cave!

"Leave me ALONE!"
snapped the bear.
"I need to SLEEP!"
And he shuffled
into the cave.

But the bear could not sleep.

Day and night,

he rolled

and rumbled.

He growled.

He howled!

"That bear sounds angry!"
cried Fox.

"What if he comes after us?"
squeaked Mouse.

"Maybe he's hungry,"
said Squirrel.

"I'll take him some food,"
said Patch. "I'm not scared
of any old bear."

Patch made a **huge** stack of blueberry
and onion sandwiches and loaded
them onto his scooter.

"Yoo-hoo, Mr. Bear!"
he called, zipping over.
"We made you a
scrumptious snack."

But Patch

forgot to look

where he was going . . . .

Suddenly, his scooter
hit a rock.

CRASH!

Down he tumbled,
right on top of the
blueberry and onion
sandwiches.

SPLAT!

From inside the cave came a terrible roar.

"Be QUIET out there!"

Bear bellowed. "Or ELSE!"

"Eeeek," squealed Mouse.
"He's coming to get us!"

"Quick!" cried Owl. "Hide!"

and walked right up to the
dark cave.

"Come back here, Hare!"
Fox called.

But Patch tiptoed closer . . . .

As Patch peeked in, he heard Bear sigh:
"I'm old and I'm cold. I'm too shivery-cold to sleep."

"He's not hungry," Patch whispered.
"He's cold. Oh, poor old bear!"

All day long, Patch couldn't stop worrying about Bear.
Finally, he lay down under a tree to think. He looked up
and saw that the leaves made a patchwork against
the evening sky. And Patch had an idea!

That night,
he tiptoed through
the forest . . .

snore

borrowing things
from all the animals.

Patch **pinned** and
stitched 'til dawn.

When the animals woke up,
they were **hopping mad.**

Just then, Patch appeared.
He spread a beautiful
patchwork quilt
on the ground.

My pajamas!

Suddenly, **Bear** stomped into the clearing.
He lifted Fox into the air.

"I SAID be QUIET!" he roared.
"I'm TRYING to SLEEP!"

The animals shook with fear—
except Patch, of course.

Patch jumped onto a stump.

"Don't be angry, Mr. Bear," he begged.

"We brought you a present—look!

It's made from clothes borrowed
from all the animals."

The old bear sniffed, then
gently set Fox down.

"You gave your things...to me?" he said.
"What fine friends you are!"

He made a quilt.

To keep you warm.

Bear clutched the cozy quilt to his furry chest,
and shuffled back into the cave.

"Hey, Mr. Bear," called Patch. "How about some
bedtime stories?"

And so, as the first flakes of snow drifted
down, the animals snuggled together
and told stories until

Bear fell

fast
asleep.